A Nickels Worth of Penny Candy

By Karen Fisher

Order this book online at www.trafford.com
or email orders@trafford.com

Most Trafford titles are also available at major online book retailers.

Printed in the United States of America.

ISBN: 978-1-4269-6854-9 (sc)

Library of Congress Control Number: 2011907047

Trafford rev. 01/06/2012

www.trafford.com

North America & international
toll-free: 1 888 232 4444 (USA & Canada)
phone: 250 383 6864 • fax: 812 355 4082

Other Trafford books for you to enjoy:

Little Miss No Feelings, Nobody, Karen Fisher

Could Have Been A Cowboy, Karen Fisher

Dedicated to Leroy and all his children

A NICKELS WORTH OF PENNY CANDY

A Nickels Worth of Penny Candy

The Man Called Harley

Being a ten year old on your own can be a scary thing. However some of the foster homes that I stayed in were just as scary. I was branded as being a mischievous prankster. I was also known as a problem child. After a short time of staying where I was sent I was often taken back to the authorities. "Trouble follows in her footsteps. We don't want her."

That was over a year ago when I ran away. I decided I would make it on my own. I wandered here and there. Staying where I found a warm safe place. I also tried above all not to be noticed.

I stole! I didn't take advantage of people. I only took what I needed. It wasn't hard to learn what I had to do in order to survive. When I was hungry I did what I could to get something to eat.

I wandered all over the place until one day I come upon this small, southeastern country town in Oklahoma. It was getting dark and when the town began to quiet down, I curled up in the entry to one of the storefronts to spend the night. It was perfect weather I wouldn't have to worry about being cold. I felt safe enough.

The sounds of the town coming to life the next morning woke me. The morning sun warmed me as it was shining in my face. I stretched and yawned. I was stiff from being curled up on the concrete. I thanked God that he helped me through another night.

Soon farmers were in town getting their supplies. Women chased their wayward children while trying to do their shopping. My stomach growled. I sure am hungry.

Trying not to draw attention to myself I walked into the store with a group of people. It was hectic and the store clerk was busy with his customers. I was carefully watching him and when he turned his back I reached for a handful of penny candy. I had a sly grin on my face as I thought I had gotten away with it one more time.

A husky hand clamped around my wrist. A booming voice said, "I wouldn't do that if I were you, baby girl. It could get you into trouble!"

I wanted to run but couldn't wiggle free from his hold. The clerk turned around and rushed over to us. "You little thief. I told you to stay out of my store!" He picked up the broom to whop me with it. I put my free arm over my face and flinched, trying to shield myself from him hitting me. I stammered in a low voice, "I-I-I was hungry...that's all."

The man that had hold of my wrist said, "Okay, Arnold put the broom away. We won't have any of that."

Arnold replied, "I want to thank you, preacher. She has stolen from me for the last time." He was walking toward the telephone while he was speaking to the preacher. "I am calling Harley. He needs to get over here and take care of this!"

I was worried how I would handle this situation when the preacher picked up an apple. "Here you are, baby girl." He smiled when I slowly took the apple from him. He slid a quarter across the counter while we waited for the man called Harley.

The preacher saw the worried look on my face. He said, "Don't worry, baby girl I am here to help you." He never once let go of me. He must have known I would bolt like a scared rabbit.

The clerk went into a rage when he saw the sheriff. "Harley, the preacher caught this winch stealing from me again! I want something done about her this time. She has taken things from me for the last time. The next time I will shoot her!"

My eyes opened wide. "Shoot me? Shoot me-because I am hungry?" My eyes filled with tears. I couldn't believe that he wanted to shoot me over a handful of penny candy. No one ever wanted to shoot me before. Who would shoot a little girl anyway?

Harley took my hand from the preacher. He must have known how upset Arnold had made me. He said, "Now hold on Arnold! No one is going to shoot anyone. Not today, not ever, not in my town!"

Harley walked me to the door, and the preacher followed. We went across the street to the sheriff's office. Harley sat me on his desk and looked at the preacher. "Well preacher, what do you think I am supposed to do about this?" Harley smiled at me. "Hello, Missy… that is your name isn't it?"

I laughed. "No-o-o that isn't my name. My name is Annie. You know like the girl with the dog! You have heard of Orphan Annie, haven't you? Cept I don't have a dog."

He looked at the preacher as I took a bite out of my big red apple. He said, "How old are you Annie?"

I wallowed the big hunk of apple in my mouth as I tried to talk. "I am ten years old."

"Where are your parents? We need let them know that we found you? I think they would be happy to know you are all right."

"No, they won't be happy. I haven't seen them for a long time. They went away. You see there is this place called Heaven and if you go there I don't think they let you come back."

They looked shocked when I said that. "Where have you been staying, Annie?" Harley asked. At first I didn't answer. My green eyes just stared at him. I blinked and said, "I stay where I can find a place that is warm and safe. I only steal when I am hungry. You won't let Arnold shoot me, will you?"Tears welled up in my eyes again at the thought of it.

Harley laughed. "No Annie, we aren't going to let Arnold shoot you." He noticed how fast I had eaten the apple the preacher bought for me. All that was left was the stem, seeds, and the hard part of the core. When he heard the growl my tummy made he telephoned the local Diner. "Helen, make me three ham sandwiches and a three Pepsi's. Bring it to the sheriff's office please, Oh and put it on my tab."

While I was busy devouring the food Helen sent over, they tried to figure out what to do. It left Harley scratching his head. I said, "Are you going to put me in jail?"

Harley laughed again. "Well, that is what I usually do with people who steal, but no little girl. You aren't going to jail."

I said, "Mister Sheriff, if you would give me food like this every day I wouldn't mind it so bad. I could get used to this real nice."Preacher and Harley laughed.

The preacher called his wife to see if she would come to Harley's office. They had five children already, but he was going to see if I could stay with them. The plan was just until they could decide what to do with me.

When preacher's wife arrived he crossed the room to tell her what was going on. She kept looking at me. Finally she said, "Don't be silly, LeeRoy of course we will take her. We can't just leave her on the streets to look out for herself.

Something would happen to her and how would we ever forgive ourselves?"

LeeRoy walked over to us. "Harley, we have decided to take her for the time being, just until we can figure out something else."

Harley jumped up and grabbed the preacher's hand. He was shaking it long and hard. He said, "Oh, that is great, preacher. It is so good to hear you say that. I had no idea what I was going to do with her."

LeeRoy took me from sitting on the desk and stood me on the floor. He took my hand and the three of us walked to their car. Harley had walked out on the sidewalk. I had my arm cupped around my large glass of Pepsi, "Good-bye, Mister Harley!" I smiled at him and he waved. "Good-bye, Annie." He had a smile on his face and he shook his head. He waved at us once more as we drove away.

Daniel And The Tigers

I sat quietly in the front seat between LeeRoy and Angelena. We were on our way to my new home. They lived in a house next to a big white church. Once we arrived there the preacher took me by the hand. I don't know why he was still doing that. I wasn't going to run anymore. A small girl about my age ran up to us. We smiled at each other.

"Hello, Papa." She giggled and squealed.

"Veanna, go round up your brothers and your sister. We are going to have a family meeting."

"All right, Papa." She darted off to tell the others about the family meeting.

We went into the house and he seated me on the sofa. Suddenly five excited children were running through the screen door. "Hello Momma! Hello Papa! Who is she?" Papa cleared his throat. "Children, I have something I want to tell you. This is Annie. She is going to be staying with us for awhile." The three boys were sad. They had another girl to put up with. Veanna was excited, but the oldest girl was unhappy like the boys. Veanna and I became friends right from the start. Teresa acted like I was intruding.

After the meeting I was whisk away by Momma Angelena to the bathroom for a scrub in the tub. As she ran me a hot bath, she told me to undress. It had been a long time since I had a bath. She handed me a bar of soap, a washcloth, shampoo, and a towel. "Wash really good, or I will have to help. I will go find one of Veanna's dresses for you to wear."

The water felt so good. I was going to come clean just from the long bath. I was having great fun soaking in the water. I already had soapy bubbles hanging from my chin when I said, "I don't wear dresses."

She turned at the door. "Papa likes his girls to look like girls. You'll get used to it."

Later Momma walked in with some clothes. I had turned from a shade of dingy gray to "squeaky clean" white. Momma said, "My, there was a little girl under all that dirt. Papa will be so surprised when he gets a look at you. I put on clean clothes. She had brought me a dress, under things, shoes, and socks. Momma brushed my long curls and put ribbons in my hair. I looked in the mirror for a long time. I couldn't ever remember looking this nice. I said, "Is that me in the mirror?"

Momma took me out for the others to see. Papa sat there with his mouth open. He said, "Baby, that can't be the same little girl you went in there with."

I smiled. Everyone laughed when I grabbed my tummy because it growled. It was always doing that. Momma had been working on dinner while I was scrubbing in the tub. The girls already set the table. Everyone ran to his or her place to sit down. I didn't know what to do, because I noticed there was no place for me. I just stood there with my head down, lost.

Papa scooted Veanna down and put a chair beside her. "Here you go, baby girl. Here is a place for you to sit." I walked over and edged my way up on the chair. Everything looked and smelled so good. My mouth was watering. I reached for a biscuit, and Papa cleared his throat. I looked at him and put it back.

"First, we say a prayer to thank the good Lord for this food and for what he has done for us today. Then you may eat." He bowed his head and prayed. Veanna giggled because just as Papa said, "Amen" my tummy growled again. It sounded like a roaring lion.

We had a good meal. We had fried chicken, potatoes, corn on the cob, and the biscuits of course. Momma was a great cook. When we were finished with our meal Papa told us girls to clean up the kitchen and do the dishes. "Annie, you can help them."

I didn't care to, but I found myself saying, "Yes sir." It was the least I could do for such a good meal.

When everything was done Papa had us come and sit around him. "What Bible story shall we read tonight?"

I joined right in and everyone began to laugh when I screamed, "Daniel and the Tigers!"Momma and Papa both smiled.

"That's Daniel and the Lions."Momma said.

I was embarrassed. "Oh, I heard about it once. I always get them mixed up."Papa opened his big black Bible and read to us just for me about Daniel and the.. .TIGERS. Lions? Tigers? Oh my. It was still fun to sit in the floor and listen to him growl like a hungry lion with his hands in the air. He was kind of scary when he did that. He told us about Daniel being thrown into the lion's den. I just didn't know how those hungry tigers didn't eat Daniel up. He said, "God helped Daniel by locking their jaws shut." LeeRoy said they couldn't have eaten him if they wanted too. You know if a tiger is hungry he is going to want to eat you.

I sure hope if I ever get thrown in a tigers' den that God will be there to help me out!

The Clashing

So far my stay of seven hours hadn't presented too many problems. We three girls went to our room to get ready for bed like they had told us to. Momma had laid my overalls in the floor when she went to find one of Veanna's dresses for me to wear. They were on Teresa's side of the room, and she didn't like it.

She bent over to pick them up. She had them pinched in between her thumb and one finger. She said in a high-pitched squeaky voice. "Yuck, these are so disgusting." She twirled around so fast, that she almost knocked me down when she bumped into me. I said, "You did that on purpose." It was evident she didn't like me and our clashing was a sure thing. I could tell that right from the start.

She said, "I did not! But if you will keep your rags on your side of the room we will get along just fine." She threw my overalls at me and they wrapped around my head. The clasp hit me in the eye. Before they hit the floor I was on top of her. We were rolling around in the floor, screaming, kicking, scratching, clawing, and pulling hair. If there was one thing I knew how to do it was how to fight. Veanna was jumping on the bed cheering me on. "Whop her Annie! Whop her!"

The door burst open. Papa demanded to know what was going on. Veanna stopped jumping on the bed and stood there not daring to move. He pulled me off of Teresa who was in tears. "Teresa, what is the meaning of all this?"

"She jumped on me!" She sobbed.

I was starting to feel I was in big trouble. Veanna yelled, "Yeah, Miss Smarty Pants, tell him why she jumped on you." I stood there figuring I would be on my way back to the authorities before the sun rose.

Teresa looked nervous like she would start crying again. Veanna kept talking. "Teresa told Annie to keep her dirty rags off her side of the room. Then she threw them at her. The buckle hit Annie in her eye. She punched at her own eye to stress the point. Why I wouldn't be surprised if she doesn't get a black eye. That is when they started fighting."

Papa said, "Veanna, I want you to go to bed. As for you two, I can see that we need to have a little talk."He motioned for Teresa to go into the living room. She walked past him. He had me by the arm at my shoulder and sort of drug me along. My pretty little hand me down black patten leather shoes barely tapped on the floor.

Teresa sat down on the sofa. LeeRoy took me by both my shoulders and lifted me up to where I was seated on the sofa. I had a huge urge to run but I dared not to. Besides where would I run? For some reason he always put the fear into me so I couldn't move. You could tell that Papa was upset by the way he was pacing the floor. Later I found out he did that when he was preaching. I think it was to help him think of what to say.

"Teresa, I am very disappointed in you. Annie is going to be a part of our family. I expected you to treat her better than this."

Teresa said, "It is just she is so-o-o dirty, and awful that-t-t. I hung my head in hurt as Papa began to scold her. I wasn't dirty and awful anymore. I stunk good now. Momma made me take a bath. Why I hadn't smelled this good in a long time.

"I am surprised at you! Annie hasn't had a home, or clothes, or food to eat half the time. I'll be the first to admit that you kids haven't had much, but you certainly had more than she has. You better let me see a change in your attitude young lady! I won't have this bickering between you. The next time I will paddle you both. Do you understand me?"

"Yes, sir." She whimpered as she burst into tears. Teresa knew she was lucky not to be getting a paddling. She was really playing the part with all the tears to try and not get one.

"All right, I want you to go to bed." He kissed her forehead and she went back to our room. I didn't know my fate with the situation. Would he be as easy on me? Should I cry? I was so scared.

"Baby girl, I know that Teresa has said some things tonight that has hurt you. When he said that I wiped away a tear from my cheek that happen to slip out of my purplish eye.

I understand that. However, as I said I will not tolerate this fighting between you. This is your first night here and I am going to let slide. I want you to feel welcome because as far as I am concerned this is your home. You are one of mine and I will treat you as such. Do you understand?"

I said a shaky "Yes sir."

"All right, you may go to bed."He kissed my forehead, and we walked down the hallway to the girls' bedroom. Momma met us at the door. She was in her robe and her long hair was falling down her back. "Good night, honey. Sleep well."

Papa echoed, "Good night, baby girl. Say your prayers, and we will see you in the morning."

I went into the room and slipped underneath the covers beside Veanna. She rolled over and whispered, "Did he whip you?"

I said a shaky "No-o-o."

Papa's voice boomed down the hall. "Veanna Mae, go to sleep!"

"Yes, Papa." She rolled over and soon was very still. I was restless. Something was stirring within me. I didn't understand why I was feeling this way. I reached up to my forehead where he had kissed me. I didn't ever remember anyone ever doing that before. I finally became tired enough to go to sleep. My last thought was what a good feeling I had being in this place.

The Widows And "Street" Orphans

With Papa being a preacher it was only a few days in their home that I learned what it was to go to church. There were two Sunday services, Wednesday services, Saturday services, and sometimes special services.

It was Sunday morning. We had cereal for breakfast and everyone was trying to dress in his or her Sunday best. The two youngest boys, Paul and Johnny were fighting over a sock. They were stretching it so far out of shape it would fit Papa before they were through. Momma finally intervened, and settled their dispute with another pair of socks.

We all filed into the church together. Papa started the service. We had three congregational songs, prayer, and announcements. Then we were going to be dismissed to our Bible classes. This part of the service was called Sunday school. I figured it was called that because you were supposed to study and learn things about the Bible. Papa said, "Before we go to our class I would like to say something. As most of you have probably already heard by the way of the town grapevine, (He liked to call it that instead of gossip) Angelena, and I have opened our home to a small girl that needed someone to love her, and to help her grow into a fine young lady."

A man interrupted Papa by standing up and shouting, "A man with five children has no business taking in another!" He was and elder in the church, and was always causing trouble.

It grew quiet and Momma was looking up as if she was asking a higher power for help. The man continued to speak. "In other words WE the church members will be supporting this street orphan."

Papa was at a loss for words at first then he said, "Sir my Bible states we are to care for the widows, and orphans. If I choose to give her a mere morsel of mine then who are you to refuse her that? I might not be eating as big a meal as I used to, because I will be sharing mine with Annie. He bent his head down and said, one of the things my mother taught me to do as a child was to share!"

Smiles began to fill the faces of the congregation. He had put this troublemaker in his place. Papa quickly said, "Let us pray." Every head bowed and a prayer was said. We were then dismissed to our classes.

In our class we had Bible stories, songs, Bible games, and prayer. It was actually fun. I did like it.

After class Veanna, and I slipped out the side door, and went next door to the house. Papa had asked Mrs. Besmears to lead the songs, and we heard them began to sing. The boys were sitting on the second row. LeeRoy began to look around the congregation for us. That is when he noticed our smiling faces missing.

He looked at Teresa and she pointed over her shoulder to the back door. Papa asked Brother Denny to take over the service until he returned. He slipped out the door at the church to retrieve us.

Veanna froze when she saw his figure standing in the door of our room. "Veanna Mae, you know better than to leave church before it is over." He put her across his knee and began to paddle her. After the spanking he sent her squalling next door. He then placed me across his knee and I got a spanking. "Baby girl, we do not leave church before it is over."

I said, “Yes sir.”I had my hand on my poor sitter. It had hurt but I didn’t cry a tear. LeeRoy had hold of my wrist, and we walked back to the church. I sat down beside Veanna, and he went on up to the front to take back charge of the service. Veanna had her head down when she said, “Did he whip you?”As she whispered she wiped away a tear.

In a trembling, shaky voice I said, “Yes-s-s!”Papa cleared his throat so we became quiet. You could tell he was in no mood for anymore misbehaving.

After church we had Sunday dinner. Veanna, Teresa, and I cleaned up the kitchen. After our chores were done Veanna, and I went and sat down on the church steps. This is a place we spent a lot of time. We usually just sat there watching the world go by. Unless of course LeeRoy was chasing us down the street for something we did.

Veanna said, “Annie, it is all my fault that Papa whipped you today. I knew how he felt about leaving church. You didn’t know he doesn’t like it.”

I said, “It sure makes you feel funny. Doesn’t it?”

She looked at me with surprise. "Funny? You can't sit down for a week, but funny? No, it doesn't make me feel funny at all."

I did feel funny. No one ever cared about me like LeeRoy seemed to. Others didn't care where I was, or what I did. But LeeRoy was so different. I almost felt like I belonged. I looked at Veanna. "I guess stealing that penny candy was the best thing I ever done."

Veanna said, "You stole candy! You better not tell Papa.... it's a sin you know!"

Ignorantly Smart

Teresa became really good to us younger kids after that first night. When LeeRoy talked with her about me she changed. She was there hovering over us like a little mother hen. Protecting us from our enemies.

She was always studying and reading books. She took time out to help us if she was needed. I never knew how she could keep up with us and read a book at the same time. If anyone would try to pick a fight she would step in to settle it. She was tall and slender for her age. That alone could be the reason things always worked out well. Everyone thought she was much older than us.

I wasn't the brightest crayon in the box. I hadn't been to school much in my young life and was very behind. She took up tutoring me trying to help me catch up. Papa encouraged me and pushed me long making sure that I stayed in school. I started with the third grade and it seemed that I had to study that much more. I wanted to make Papa proud of me. To make him think I was worth the trouble. When I was with my mother she would say, "You are more trouble than you're worth."Every time I turned around I could hear her saying that in my head. "You are nobody and you aren't worth the trouble."I was very young then. I remember I used to think why does my mom hate me so much? I'm not such a bad kid. I cried myself to sleep a lot.

I think I become so overwhelmed by all the work and learning so much at one time that I began to lose interest in school. It wasn't as fun as it had been in the beginning. In fact I started to hate school. I was caught daydreaming over and over again. I would get in trouble a hundred times a day. The first time I skipped school I found myself in big trouble with LeeRoy.

We walked to school together in the morning. This morning my siblings complained about my dragging my feet. "If you don't come on we are going to be late for school."Even Veanna was aggravated at me.

Don said, "Let's just run off and leave her. It would serve her right. She can walk to school by herself!" He knew

LeeRoy would be mad for leaving one of us alone but he was too upset at the time to care.

I bent down to tie my shoe. The others just kept walking on without me. Once they went around the bend in the road I picked up my lunch and books. I ran straight toward the creek bank. I sat under the big shade tree close to the water. I made me a fishing pole out of string, a stick, and the hook I had stuck in my ball cap. I found some worms under a log. Fishing was my favorite thing to do.

LeeRoy knew that. He loved to eat fish. I loved to catch fish. It reminded me of the time Veanna and I went to catch him a fish dinner. We fished all day and didn't get any bites. When I took in my line to go home I had a fish that was two inches wide and about three inches long. "Hot dog! Let's take this fish to Papa for dinner."

We had a big tub of water. I was screaming for LeeRoy to come and see our fish that we caught for him. The fish was in my hand and I was splashing water all over the yard like it was a whopper. I held up that little fish and he let out a scream the whole block could hear. We couldn't help but laugh. He would chase us down the street when we would pull pranks on him. All the neighbors would say, "Annie and Veanna must be in trouble, Preacher is chasing them down the street again."It wasn't long our story got out through the town grapevine. When my friend Ronnie's dad heard about it he said, "Here is the girl that paid tithes with her fish. She brought the pastor a tenth of a fish."

About noon a voice behind me said, "Well, what are you doing here?"Startled from thinking about my fish story, I turned around to find Ronnie standing there. He had missed me at school and came looking for me.

"What does it look like? I am trying to catch some fish!"

He plopped down beside me in the shade and said, "You know if they catch us we will be in trouble."When he said that he took the other hook out of my hat and made me share my string.

I said, "I know that, but I couldn't sit through another one of Mr. Dunn's classes. That wasn't the real reason. You don't have to stay if you are scared. Go back to school, you big wuss."

He had a sly grin on his face. We sat talking about things, and shared my lunch. Royal was the class bully. He was the subject of our conversation. Royal was hateful and loved to pick on me. Ronnie was jealous and always wanted to pound him for it. He frowned at me and said, "I hate how he gives you so much trouble." I could tell Ronnie liked me. We had something special right from the start. I liked him also. It was like we had chemistry. We would just smile into each other's eyes a certain I like you way. The first time I saw him I looked at him like that.

Ronnie said, "You know Annie, You are pretty swell for a girl."

I smiled at him. I knew the reason he liked me was because I was more of a tomboy. I liked to do guy things like fishing, climbing trees and I could run like an antelope. I pushed him and said, "Oh shut up all that mushy stuff. I like you too, but you don't hear me telling you, do you?"

He laughed and said, "I think you just did."

We had just made clear our feelings for each other when someone grabbed us. I was screaming for Ronnie to help me, but they had captured him also. Mr. Simmons, and Mr. Hamm were taking us to Harley for playing hooky. Harley called Papa. It seemed like he knew his telephone number by heart. I was really nervous when Papa pushed the door to the sheriff's office open. He talked to Harley. He took care of matters and we left for home.

I was truly hoping he wouldn't give me a whipping. I had a few from him and I didn't want anymore. He was silent all the way home, which made me all the more scared of him. I walked into the house and sat down on the edge of the couch. I was looking at my feet afraid to look at him. He sat down across from me. In his booming scary voice he said, “All right, young lady, we are going to talk. What is this skipping school today all about?”

I swallowed hard as a lump the size of a silver dollar swelled up inside my throat. I didn’t know what to say to him and I still hadn’t looked at him.

“Annie, I am really disappointed in you.”

“Yes, sir.”I whispered.

He said, “Aren’t you even going to explain to me what the reason for this is?”

I had tears in my eyes. “Because I’m not very smart you know.”

“What does that mean Ann?”

“It means that I must be a big dummy just like Royal says I am.”By now I was sobbing and really feeling sorry for myself. Poor, poor Annie!

LeeRoy said, “Did Royal really say that you were dumb?”

"Yes, he did. He said I was a dump little tramp and you only took me in because you felt sorry for me. I thought you took me in because you loved me like the other children." Tears still running down my face.

"Ann, I did feel sorry for you, but because you didn't have anyone to help you grow into a beautiful young lady. At the rate you were going you would have never made it. I do love you as much as the other children and Momma and I try to show you that every day. You do like it here, don't you Annie?"

"Oh! Yes sir, I really do."

He smiled when I said that. It was quiet then he said, "Well, what did you do about Royal?"

He would have to ask me that. I studied his face and swallowed hard again. "I socked him right in the eye." I took my fist and shoved it in the air imitating socking Royal in the eye.

He said, "Was that the right thing to do?"

I said, "At the time I thought it was, but, no, sir it wasn't. That is why I didn't go to school today. I knew that Mr. Blankenship would call me into his office. I knew he wouldn't understand. I thought it would be best if I avoided it all together."

He said, "Annie, even if the others make better grades than you I want you to know that I will be proud of you as long as I know that you have done your best. You will go back to school tomorrow!"

"Yes sir, I guess I will."

He said, "I know you will, and I better not hear of you missing classes anymore. Do you understand me, young lady?"

"Yes Sir."

"As for Royal, there will be no need for anymore eye punching."

I said, "You don't know Royal very well!" He gave me a look so I quickly said, "Yes sir."

Wouldn't you know a week later they had a spelling bee for the third grade. It was so nerve racking. It was a weird twist of fate but at the end there were only two contestants standing. Royal was one of them! I was the other! I couldn't believe it? I was sweating like a pig. (I know that pigs don't sweat, but this little pig was sweating badly.)

We volleyed words back and forth while all our parents watched the competition. It was becoming quite a match. I spelled the next word wrong. Royal would get a chance to spell it. If he spelled it correct, he would be the champion of the spelling bee. I stood there rocking back and forth on my feet as he gave it a try. How could I have missed my word?

He got it right! He was the winner! I was the loser! I had tears in my eyes and walked toward Royal. Papa sat straight up in his chair not knowing what to expect from me. My fist was clinched and I had tears rolling down my face. When I got to Royal he was standing there frozen from fear. It looked as if he thought I was going to punch him in the eye. I held out my hand to shake his. He threw his hands over his face to protect himself. When I didn't hit him, he looked through his fingers. He finally reached out his hand and shook my hand. I ran off the stage in tears. The loss was devastating, but I had done my very best. I had almost won. I didn't like being an almost winner.

Papa didn't care that I had lost. He knew that I tried really hard. He even thought that it was worth an ice cream cone at the diner. That chocolate ice cream was the best I remember ever tasting.

Cousin Ben

Veanna and I always got bored real easy. Papa always tried to never let that happen because it was dangerous. He always said, "What one won't think of, the other one will."

We were laying on our bed when I said, "To bad we can't go outside."

Veanna said, "Why?"

"I have fireworks. We could have fun with them if we could go outside."

Veanna said, "We couldn't have fun with them outside. Someone would call Harley. Especially at two o'clock in the morning." She was right, but we were still teasing each other about the fireworks. Suddenly Veanna said, "Let's pop them in here!"

I shook my head and said, "I don't think we can't do that. We could catch the house on fire?" The whole time I was placing a black cat firecracker in the middle of the hallway floor. Veanna struck the match. I was thinking there is no way under God's blue heaven that Veanna will light this firecracker in the house at two o'clock in the morning!

Sparks started flying everywhere in the hallway. I screamed, "Veanna!"We took off running, jumped in our bed, and threw the covers over our head as the firecracker exploded.

Momma yelled, "Veanna Mae, WHAT WAS THAT?'

"It was a fire cracker, Momma."

Momma said, "You two save the fire works for outside or I am going to get up and show you a few fireworks!"

"All right Momma."Papa hadn't even moved or yelled at us. He must have slept right through it.

The next evening we had a big surprise. Just about sun down Papa's nephew stopped in for a visit. He was from California and had walked most of the way here. He had a backpack and a bedroll on his back. LeeRoy was going to let him stay in his home for a while. He told him he would be in the boy's bedroom with them.

After a few months Veanna and I got used to him being there. We didn't like the way he wanted to control us even though he was older than us. He liked to boss us around.

One Friday morning Momma was going to drive Veanna and I to Grandma's farm to spend the night. She lived about eight miles from town. So every once in a while we would take her groceries, clean her house, do her laundry, mow the lawn, and do anything else she needed done.

The next morning Veanna called Momma to tell her we were going to walk over to Ronnie's house to visit. If she wanted us that is where we would be. Veanna began to argue over the telephone with momma. "If you send Ben after us, we won't ride home with him!" Momma said, "What is wrong with Ben coming after you?"

Veanna said, "I just don't want to ride with him, Momma. If you send him after us we won't come home."

She hung up the telephone. We said good-bye to Grandma and walked to Ronnie's house. The walk was great. It was spring. The grass was green, the flowers were blooming and the birds were singing. Everything smelled so good and clean. Except the cows of course, they didn't smell so sweet. I was watching for snakes though. I didn't want to step on another one of those. Once at Ronnie's house we noticed his dad Ernest was plowing a garden spot.

We played a game of Horseshoes until Ernest got the soil just the way he wanted it. When he had it ready we helped him plant tomatoes, onions, beans, corn, squash, carrots and cucumbers. They had a big garden. They had a big family and his mother would can everything they grew. Ernest appreciated our help and after everything was planted we started a new game of Horseshoes.

We heard the sound of our old car coming up the hill to Ronnie's farm. I said, "Well, it sounds as if Momma has come to get us."When the car pulled up to the house, there sat Ben behind the wheel. He sat there smiling as he parked the car, probably because we were looking at him.

Veanna was in a rage when she saw him. "We aren't ready to go home yet so you can turn the car around and leave!" Ben got out of the car and come over to where we were standing.

Ronnie said, “If she talked to me that way I would pick me a switch.”He always said that when we got sassy.

Ben said, “If they were my girls I wouldn’t let them get away with half the things they do! He didn’t even take a breath when he said, “It doesn’t matter if you aren’t ready to go home yet! I have come after you. So I am telling you to go GET in the car.”

Veanna said, “I am not getting in the car! I told Momma we wouldn’t come home if she sent you after us. So we are not going!”

Ben looked my direction. I was just quietly minding my own business. “Both of you go to the car!” He was pointing at the car without even looking at it. “I am not kidding Annie. I mean it!”

Veanna knew I would probably wimp out and do as he said so she stepped between Ben and me. “I said we are not going home with you! Can’t you get that through your thick head?”

That made Ben mad. He turned around and went to the car. He said, “You’re going to be sorry when your mother comes back after you.” He slammed the door. As he was going down the hill he was screaming out the window. "You are going to be sorry!"

Veanna laughed like it didn't bother her, but I was a little bit worried. Ronnie looked at me and said, "It looks as if you are going to have a long walk back to town!" I smiled, but I didn't know what we were going to do. How would we get home? I sure didn't want to walk eight miles. Ernest said, "Naw, Ya'll ain't gonna to walk to town. Somebody would kidnap you. Ronnie will take you to town here in a bit."

Ronnie said, "Now, daddy, you know good and well if anyone took these girls they would surely turn them loose after they were around them any time at all." By the look on Ronnie's face he wasn't thrilled about taking us to town. It was enough to make me laugh at him.

We went over and continued our game of Horseshoes. We were having a great time when we heard the car coming back up the hill. I said, "Well, it sounds like Ben is back."

Ronnie said, "Oh, no, it isn't Ben. It is your mother and she is mad.

Momma got out of the car. She wasn't happy with us at all. "What is the meaning of you not coming home when I sent Ben all the way out here? I didn't feel well. I didn't want to drive all the way out here. Go get in the car! I am so mad at you both! Just wait until I get you home. I am going to give you twenty lashes apiece!"You could tell she wasn't kidding. You could almost see smoke coming out of her ears.

It sounded like a joke, but I knew she was serious because she was furious. It embarrassed me because Ronnie was grinning. He said, "Make that Twenty-two lashes!"

I said, "Shut up, Ronnie!"When I was started to the car I gave him a bit of a shove.

Ronnie's mother, Mae was standing on the porch and said, "Well, if you whip Veanna, whip Annie too."

I didn't want to tell Ronnie's mother to shut up so I said, "Be quiet!"They were all laughing and waving good-bye as we drove down the hill. Ronnie looked at his mother and said, "I think those two girls are in trouble.

Veanna and I were trying to get Momma to laugh all the way home, but she wouldn't hear of it. Halfway home she was still mad so I figured we would get twenty lashes apiece once we got home! Hopefully it wouldn't be twenty-two like Ronnie had suggested. How were we going to get out of this situation? I have to do some quick thinking.

Bossy Brothers

When we were home and turned into the drive a strange car was sitting there. Papa's nephew Louie and his wife were here from California. They were looking for Ben. Everyone got out of the cars and began to hug each other. I looked at Veanna. We both knew Louie had just saved our hides. I would much rather have hugs than lashes. Louie was Ben's older brother. I never met him, but I was sure was glad to see him.

Momma sent Veanna and I to the store to get something for dinner. Papa worked in the back of the grocery store at the meat market. He was waiting on a customer when he looked up and saw us walk into the store.

"What is this I hear about you two not coming home?" His voice boomed.

We heard him at the front of the store. I looked up at the ceiling and said, "Did you hear that?"

Papa started around the counter and was wiping his hands on his apron. He started toward us. "I ought to paddle you both."

I said, "LeeRoy, don't get excited."We hurried around the store grabbing what we needed for dinner so we could go before Papa caught us. Our neighbors were buying their groceries. They were laughing because Veanna and I were in trouble. They saw LeeRoy chasing us down the street on a daily basis. Now he was chasing us down the aisles in the grocery store.

We went home and cooked dinner for Momma. Papa finally came home from work. Veanna was mad and was trying to throw the boys out of the kitchen. She was having a hard time doing it and making quite a squabble about it. There was a lot of screaming, fussing, and wrestling. The boys didn't want to go just because she wanted them too.

Louie became tired of all the noise and grabbed Veanna. He said, "Uncle LeeRoy, when is the last time you gave this one a spanking?" Louie felt she needed one because she was being so loud.

Papa said, "It has been a while. However, the other night when that firecracker went off in the house at two o'clock in the morning I almost took my belt to both of them."

We were shocked because this was the first time he had mentioned the firecracker. He hadn't slept through it like we thought.

Louie looked over toward me. I was just sitting there minding my own business as usual. "How about this one? Has she had a spanking lately?"

I just looked at him like he better leave me alone. You could tell he was Ben's older brother. He was just as bossy as Ben was.

I was so glad when Veanna announced that dinner was ready. At least if nothing else it changed the subject.

Girlfriend Gayle

Veanna and I were growing up. The day Veanna had been waiting for was finally here. She was able to get her driver's license. We had been saving our money together in hopes of getting us a clunker car. It was old but in fairly good shape. Most importantly, it ran good.

Here in this part of the country the kids always learned to drive the back roads from the time you are twelve. So we practically knew all there was to driving a car. You just couldn't drive on the highway until you could get your license. We were always running here and there. Papa practically gave up on trying to keep up with us.

That year I met a girl I liked as a friend. Gayle lived down the dirt road from Ronnie's house. What really astounded me about her was there were twelve children in her family. She was the only girl. How can there be twelve children and only one girl? You would think she would be quite spoiled, but her mother was a very jealous person. She didn't treat her very well.

Mrs. Maxine made her scrub the floors, do the laundry, cook the meals, and wash the dishes. It was like she was a slave to the household. It was such a Cinderella story.

When I became her best friend we always found fun without even looking for it. There was a preacher at another church that was like a father figure to Gayle. She really liked him and his wife. They treated her like a daughter. I think she liked that because she didn't get any good attention at home.

This was all good and well, but Preacher Charles didn't like me. I didn't care much for him. He didn't like Gayle running around with me. He thought I was a bad influence on her. He was a strict preacher. His sermons were the fire and brimstone kind. He didn't like that I liked to swim at the pits, or the fact that I wore jeans most of the time, and that I liked to go to football games. He thought it was a sin to go to football games.

Preacher Charles looked at me and said, "If you didn't have your jeans on you could go to visitation with me." I always knew he was talking to me because I was the one wearing the jeans. He would shake his head in disapproval.

I said to him, "Who says I want to go to visitation with you?" Gayle would grin because she knew I didn't want to go with him. If papa knew I talked to him that way I would be in big trouble. It wasn't showing respect. He was hateful to me so I would be hateful to him right back.

He would scowl at me and say, "I don't like you girls swimming down at the pits. I saw bear's tracks there the other day and she has a cub. It is really dangerous for you to be there. If that bear came upon you she probably would attack. Then what would you do?"

I never heard of bears in the area and I figured he was just trying to keep us away from the water hole. I should have known it could be true because there were lots of trees on the mountainside, and wild animals running around.

I told Grammy about it and was laughing she said, "Well, there could very well be a bear at those old pits. A bear got into Sable's pig pen last year and he was into all kinds of trouble over killing it."

Every time Gayle and I got together she wanted to go visit the Preacher. I went along with her because that is what best friends do. I went even though he would probably gripe at me the whole time. We walked in the house and his wife was standing in the kitchen doing the dishes. Gayle said, "Where is the Preacher at?"His wife Lou said, "He is down the hill gathering the eggs."

Gayle and I walked right out the back door without even stopping. Since it was getting dusky dark we could see the Preacher coming up the trail between the trees. He was carrying two-dozen eggs in his arms. Gayle saw him about the same time I did. He hadn't noticed us yet and she shoved me behind a tree. What in the world is she doing?

When preacher went walking past us, Gayle jumped out from behind our tree and screamed so loudly that it echoed back to us from the hills. The Preacher jumped from being frightened and smashed all the eggs against him. They ran down his shirt and dripped off his arms. His whole baldhead and his ears turned red from being so mad. I was laughing at him so much I could hardly breathe. Gayle said, "Ahh Preacher, you kinda broke all your eggs there."

I just about lost it. I had tears rolling down my face from laughing so hard. Of course I didn't tell anyone but she scared me too. Only I didn't have eggs to break.

We went to Ronnie's house. All I could see was Preacher Charles with eggs running down him. I couldn't quit laughing. Ronnie mom said, "What on earth does she keep laughing about?"

When Gayle started to tell our story the others were laughing too. That is everyone except Ronnie. He just had a solemn look on his face. He said, "If I were the Preacher I would have picked a switch off that tree." He didn't think the preacher breaking his eggs was funny. He just didn't understand. The preacher had griped at me so much I just felt it was payback. I think that is why I thought it was so great. You just can't get back at someone any better than that. It was a priceless moment for me.

Church Camp

Being in the denomination we were in, they were a strict church. They had church camp every year for all the kids in the state of Oklahoma. Papa being one of the pastors arranged for the children in his church to be there. It meant we did a lot of fundraisers to raise the money for everyone to go.

We had bake sales, car washes, took donations, baby-sit, the guys mowed lawns. We basically did any chore we could do to get enough money.

The campgrounds was in Sapulpa Oklahoma. It would take us two hours to get there. Papa really had his hands full with a busload of teenagers.

Once we got there the girls grabbed all their things and went to find a bed in the girls dorm. The boys went in the other direction to find a bed in the boy's dorm.

We were on our own after that. There was breakfast in the morning, church services, lunch, recreation, rest, dinner, then church services in the evening. Then we had to be in the dorms for bedtime. That was the schedule everyday for the whole week.

There were about twelve counselors from all the different churches in the state. There were about two hundred kids from all over Oklahoma. We made a lot of new friends during the week.

I told the boys to make all the counselors welcome if they knew what I meant. That night they put one of the first time counselors in the showers with his clothes on. When he ran out of there they hit him with a torn pillow. Feathers stuck to him and he looked like a chicken. He was running all over the campus. It was so funny. Every day they would tell us what had happened in the dorm. The men counselors were asking me to keep my big mouth shut. They didn't like any of my ideas. The next night one of the boys sprayed a whole can of shaving cream on the young counselor. He was running around the campus and looked like a snowman.

I had a suitcase full of booby trap firecrackers and we tied one on the bathroom door. When someone would open the door it would pop. Veanna said, “Did you hear that?”

I said. “Yes I did.’

She said, “How will we know who got it?”

I said, “We won’t have to say anything, because we will hear who it was.”

At breakfast the next day the young counselor was telling his wife what had happened to him the night before. She said, “You think that is bad, I went to the rest room and a firecracker went off in my face. I almost wet my pants. I thought someone had shot me.”

About five of us girls started to laugh and she said, “I think I just found out who did it.”

Veanna and my name were on the KP list every day. That was the list you were put on when you did something wrong. It meant you had to report to the kitchen and do chores.

Something like peel tons of potatoes, do dishes for the whole camp, or pick up trash on the campus.

They would always find something for you to do for your sins. Frankie one of the older counselors would walk around with a clipboard writing down names. We would be in a group of about ten people and when he would walk up we would all scatter. He would be left standing there by himself looking around to see where everyone went. One day when I reported for KP I was told to make hamburgers. The line was moving smoothly when I saw Papa, he hollered out before he got to where we were. "Don't let her touch my hamburger."

The counselor standing there was just as ornery as I was. She put a crumb of meat, a small chunk if onion, and one small pickle. She wrapped it up and handed it to him. He was a happy camper that she had made it for him.

When he sat down to eat and opened his hamburger you could hear him yell all the way from the back of the room. "She has done it to me again!"

When in fact I hadn't done it to him again. But he just knew I had something to do with it. The next church service my name was on the list for KP.

John was the man in charge over KP. KP meaning of course Kitchen Patrol. I walked up to him and began to follow him around talking the whole time. He was carrying his ball bat around.

I said, "John, I had KP yesterday. If you don't believe me you can just ask Mrs. Martin. She knows I was there and you can ask LeeRoy. He can tell you that I had KP. I just don't think it is fair for me to have it again when there are a lot of kids here that hasn't had the pleasure to have it yet. To be in here with you in this lovely kitchen doing all it is that you do. So if you don't mind I would just love it if you would find someone else besides me to fill this space. It would be so much better if you would please do that for me."The more he tried to get away from me the more I followed him, and the more I talked.

Finally he turned around and said, "Will you shut up and get out of here!"

I said, "That is all I wanted to hear from you."I smiled at the man standing beside him and said, "I sure am glad he gave in I was running out of thing to say!"

That night after the service and in between the time that we had before bedtime we were walking around the campus visiting with everyone. I had a little rubber snake in my hand. The camp speaker saw it and said, "Give me that!"

After he had taken it away from me he threw it at one of the big fat lady counselors. She started dancing around, screaming hysterically, and flapping her arms like a bird. Everyone was laughing at her.

When the speaker had walked away she said, "How can I get back at him?"

I said, "I have a booby trap firecracker."

She said, "Go get it for me."So I did. She knew which room he was staying in and she tied it on his door. She said, "One of you go tell him his little boy has woke up crying so he will come to his room."

Gayle ran to tell him the news. We were watching him run all across the campus going to his room. He slung the door open and KaPow!!!!!!!! The firecracker went off. He fell back against the hallway wall and just slid down to the floor.

The fat counselor took off through the campus laughing and saying, "Guess what I just did to the camp speaker."

He said, "What can I do to get her back?"

I said, "I have another booby trap."

He said, "Go get it for me."

I loved it. We were having loads of fun and not getting in trouble or being put on the KP list. I think I just figured out how to work this.

I had a copper wire tube that wrapped around in a circle with the end pointing back at you. I had a straight piece in the middle with holes drilled in it. I had filled it with powder and was just carrying it around waiting for the right person to ask me about it. John said, "What do you have there?"

I said, "It is a bird call."He said, "Oh yeah, what kind of birds can you call with it?"

"Just about any kind that you want to I guess."

He said, "Let me try it."

I said, “No, you don’t want to try it.”

He said, “Come on let me try it.”

I finally gave in to him. He took it and went to the door of the lunchroom. He was looking up in the trees to see what kind of birds there were.

Then he did it! He blew into that horn and all the powder went all over his face. He blew powder out of his mouth and was trying to clear it out of his hair and eyes. I just stood there looking at him. One of the girls standing there said, “She told you not to do it.”

We had a great time at church camp and it was great finding out there were other kids out there that were just like us.

LeeRoy was sure that it did some of the kids good. He just didn’t know if it helped all of us.

The Pokey

Veanna and I were always in our clunker car going somewhere. One night we were running around and we ended up in Bokoshe. I screamed, "Veanna STOP! There is Ronnie's truck at the cafe."

We parked in a space close by. There were five boys standing on the sidewalk in front of the establishment. They were yelling at us when I said, "Hey, do you know if Ronnie is in the Cafe?"

The one young cowboy said, "Well, now Missy I do believe he is."

I said, "Would you mind asking him to come out here? We want to talk to him."

The young cowboy stuck his body halfway in the Cafe door and hollered, "Hey, Ronnie there are a couple of good-looking girls out here. They want to talk to you! You are one lucky man, my friend."

Ronnie looked out of the door to the diner. He was holding a pool stick. He handed it to his friend, and walked out to see what we wanted. He came over to our car and said, "What are you two doing?"

"We were out running around and I happened to see your truck. What are you doing?"

"Well, I was playing a game of pool. For once I was winning until you interrupted me."

The young cowboy strolled over to our car and said, "Hello, ladies. Ronnie is so rude he didn't even introduce you to me. My name is Johnnie."He had his thumbs tucked into the front of his jeans, but he took one of them out to tip his hat to us.

I was thrilled because I had never had a guy tip his hat to me. He said, "I do believe that I know you from somewhere. I just can't place where I met you before."

Veanna and I began to tease him. Veanna said, "I know. You are in our auto mechanics class in Vo-tech."

Ronnie, Veanna, and I grinned because he was taking it all in. She said, "Just ask us a question about cars and we can tell you all about it."

The young cowboy scratched his head under his cowboy hat and said, "Let me see now." He asked a question about his car. We gave him the answer.

Every time he asked a question one of us knew the answer. About that time the sheriff was driving down the one street town. I was scared of him because I heard he was mean. He wasn't at all as nice as Harley.

He saw the crowd and began to show out in front of all the boys. He peeled out in his police car. It was evident these boys were not scared of him. They began to whoop, holler, and say, "Here pig, pig." The Sheriff did a U-turn laying rubber, spraying smoke, and gravel all the way around. He pulled up where everyone was standing. He was driving so fast I thought he was going to run right through the Cafe.

I was petrified. He jumped out of his squad car and was walking toward the crowd. He had his hand in the air pointing at us. "You get out of here! You walk. You run. You crawl. You get out of here!" He gestured like an umpire would at a ball game when he yells you're out.

Veanna started the car and said, "See you later, Ronnie."

He said, “No, don’t go. He isn’t going to do anything about it.”The sheriff got back into his car and peeled out backwards. Again leaving smoke and rubber. It looked to me like he was egging the boys on and it worked. When he did that the boys started making piggy sounds and yelling pig, pig again. Veanna and I were leaving this time. I could just see us needing to call LeeRoy to come get us out of jail. Ronnie got in his truck and followed us out of town.

When we got on the dirt road to the turn out we stopped the car. We got out of our vehicles. Ronnie was laughing at me and he said, “What is the matter? Did that scare you?”

“Yes, he scared me! I could see us calling Papa to get us out of jail. Wouldn’t that scare you?”

Ronnie knew Papa and he said, “Yeah, I think that would have scared even me.”

“He would have beat us into next week!”Veanna said.

I told Ronnie, “You guys are crazy to take on that sheriff. I have always heard he is bad.”

Ronnie said, "Oh, he is a pussycat, but it probably was a good idea that we left when we did."

We got in Ronnie's truck and went to Spiro since we were close by. Everyone knew us here. All the kids were driving around through town. It was a one street town too. All the parking spaces were in the middle of the street. We would drive the length of the shops and at the end of town we would turn at the intersection and go the other way. It was known as the circle.

One of the boys we went to school with put a box over his head. He cut places out for his arms to stick out. We knew who it was, but he couldn't be recognized because the box was over his head. He was walking up and down the streets clowning around. He would walk like a duck or Charlie Chaplin. He even had a cane. Everyone was honking and laughing at him. He walked right up to Harley's office and knocked on the window with the cane.

Harley came out and got him by the arm and took him into his office. I think they thought he was naked under the box because his pant legs were rolled up. All you could see was the box, hairy legs, and cowboy boots. I looked at Ronnie. "Are they going to arrest him?"Ronnie said, "It sure looks that way."All the kids in the whole town got upset. There were about fifty cars circling the town. Horns were honking as they went passed Harley's office.

I told Ronnie, "What is it with tonight? Get us out of here. Take us to our car so we can go home. I am not calling LeeRoy tonight to come get us out of jail."Veanna and I went home. After all it was getting late.

The next day LeeRoy pointed to his gray hair and said, "See this? See these? Veanna and Annie put every one of these in my hair." Of course there were a lot of things he didn't know about us. All of his hair would be gray. For instance almost being in jail last night.

He was right though. What one wouldn't think of, the other one did. I found a cigar box in Mr. Terry's trash barrel. I rescued it because I had great plans for this special box.

I cut a hole in the front of it. I put mousetrap hinges on the lid to put pressure on it. I put a latch on it to hold the lid shut. Then I put a screened in porch on the front of it. I tied a rubber snake on a string and put it inside the box. When you would get someone close enough to look in the hole in the box you would just trip the latch and the lid would fly open and sling the snake on the string out at the person looking in the box. It would scare everyone. They would scream and run away. Then they would laugh and say let me see that. They would go try it on someone they knew.

After we tried it on LeeRoy and after everything calmed down he was giving me a talking too. I said, "Not all of these things were my fault LeeRoy."

He said, "No. Whose idea was it about the firecracker?"

"Mine."

"Whose idea was it about the fish?"

"Mine."

"Now whose idea was it about the snake?"

"Mine."

"And who should be in trouble for all this shenanigans?"

"Veanna," I said.

Lee Roy burst into laughter. Every once in a while I could get him to laugh. He was such a fun person to pick on. I just have one thing to say. We didn't like being in trouble. We sure liked the attention we got from him, which was about every day. "Preachers, you got to love em."